JINKS ALIENS

THE VERRUCA BAZOOKA

Collect all the books in the *GUNK Aliens* series!

JONNY MOON

GUNK ALIENS

THE VERRUCA BAZOOKA

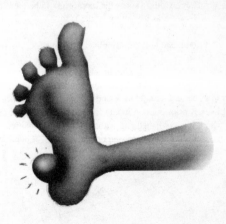

HarperCollins *Children's Books*

First published in paperback in Great Britain by HarperCollins *Children's Books* 2009
HarperCollins *Children's Books* is a division of HarperCollins*Publishers* Ltd
77-85 Fulham Palace Road, Hammersmith, London W6 8JB

The HarperCollins website address is:

www.harpercollins.co.uk

1

ISBN: 978-0-00-731094-4

Printed and bound in England by Clays Ltd, St Ives plc

Special thanks to Colin Brake,
GUNGE agent extraordinaire.

A long time ago, in a galaxy far, far away, a bunch of slimy aliens discovered the secret to clean, renewable energy...

... snot!

(Well, OK, clean-*ish*.)

There was just one problem. The best snot came from only one kind of creature.

Humans.

And humans were very rare. Within a few years, the aliens had used up all the best snot in their solar system.

That was when the Galactic Union of Nasty Killer Aliens (GUNK) was born. Its mission: to find human life and drain its snot. Rockets were sent to the four corners of the universe, each carrying representatives from the major alien races. Three of those rockets were never heard from again. But one of them landed on a planet quite simply *full* of humans.

This one.

CHAPTER ONE

It started like any other Saturday, but for Jack Brady this particular weekend was the beginning of an adventure he would never forget.

Little realising that he was destined for greatness, Jack woke up, went to the loo, washed his face and hands and cleaned his teeth. Jack was a very clean nine-year-old boy.

He was also very clever. A genius, in fact. Only no one else seemed to have noticed.

At school he got into trouble for drawing sketches of his latest inventions all over his exercise books. At home Mum just wanted him to keep his room tidy. In his heart, however, Jack knew that it was just a matter of time before his genius was recognised.

He slipped on his glasses and took a look at the 'TO-DO LIST' pinned on his notice board.

1. COMPLETE CANINE SCUBA DEVICE.

2. DRAW UP BLUEPRINTS FOR AUTOMATIC TOAST BUTTERER.

3. SOLVE WORLD ENERGY PROBLEM (IF TIME BEFORE TEA).

He shook his head in annoyance. He *never* got round to the last item on his list. There just weren't enough hours in the day!

Oscar thought Jack was a genius. Oscar was Jack's best friend. He was taller than Jack, braver than Jack and better-looking than Jack but he wasn't *smarter* than Jack. In fact sometimes Jack wondered if Oscar was actually a bit dim. He was certainly courageous though – he was always first to volunteer to be a crash-test dummy for Jack's latest invention.

Thinking of Oscar made Jack frown and check his watch. It was Saturday morning. Eight o'clock. Why hadn't Oscar come round? Most kids, after a long, boring week at school would choose to lie in on Saturday morning. But not Oscar. Oscar didn't like to waste a single *minute* of the weekend.

Normally he was up before Jack, planning some kind of adventure. So where was he?

Oscar lived in the house that backed onto Jack's garden. They shared a den – a tree house – perched in the branches of the tree at the bottom of Oscar's garden. From Jack's bedroom he could see into Oscar's house.

Jack opened his bedroom window.

THWACK!

"Ouch!" exclaimed Jack.

"Sorry!" came an apologetic voice from the tree-house opposite.

Whatever Oscar had thrown at him had lodged in Jack's unruly mop of hair. He reached up to see what it was. It was small, ovoid and very hard.

"Why are you throwing acorns at me?" he demanded.

"Because I couldn't find any pebbles," said Oscar, as if the answer was obvious. "Come on," he continued, "climb down the drainpipe and let's get started."

Jack leaned out of the window and cast a suspicious glance at the drainpipe. "Since when do I climb down drainpipes?" he asked.

"Got to be a first time for everything," grinned Oscar. "*I'd* do it."

Yes, thought Jack, *but you'd stick your head in the oven to see if the gas was still on.* "I'll be there in a minute," he promised, and closed the window.

Having taken the safer option – the stairs – he hurried through the kitchen and out into the garden, squeezed through the gap in the hedge that separated the two plots and climbed up the wooden ladder that was fixed to the trunk of the tree.

The tree house the boys shared was pretty impressive. Oscar's dad had won it in a competition in the local paper. It was actually a small shed that had been lifted into place by a crane and secured safely to the tree. It had a little porch area at the front, a pair of windows and room for Jack's workbench where most of his brilliant ideas took shape. It was, without doubt, the coolest tree house in town.

Jack found Oscar lying on a beanbag, clutching a skateboard to his chest. Oscar sighed loudly and theatrically as Jack, slightly breathless from the climb, came into the tree house.

"Good afternoon," he sighed.

"Hilarious," said Jack.

Oscar was always like this – everything had to happen *right now*. Jack felt that most things that were worth doing needed proper planning and preparation. But for Oscar if it wasn't instant it wasn't interesting.

"What's the plan then?" asked Jack, sitting down in the other beanbag.

"Mum got me this," said Oscar, holding up the skateboard. "But it doesn't go fast enough." He sat up with a wild look in his eyes. "So I thought… you could maybe fit it with some rockets. Or, you know, something..."

Jack stared. "You want me to put *rockets* on your skateboard? Why? So you can do an ollie into orbit?"

Oscar stopped to consider this – for half a second. "Could you?" he asked.

"No," said Jack firmly. "Hurtling at high speed into brick walls might be your idea of fun, but I prefer to spend my time working on my gadgets."

He got up and went over to his workbench, where a number of projects were underway. He picked up a dog-shaped rubber suit which had twin silver tubes running down its back. "See this," he announced proudly, "it's a scuba kit for a dog. Now man's best friend doesn't have to sit by and wait when you go for a scuba dive."

"You don't have a dog," Oscar pointed out.

"Well, no," agreed Jack, "but I'd like to."

"And you don't scuba dive," continued Oscar.

"Er… no. But—"

"You'd like to?"

Jack shot Oscar a dirty look. "Not really," he confessed. "It looks a bit dangerous."

Oscar sighed again. If it wasn't a bit dangerous then what was the point?

"What else have you got then? There must be something we can have fun with."

"There's the heli-frisbee," offered Jack. "I was thinking that it's really annoying that I can't ever throw a Frisbee properly so I designed a Frisbee that even I can use."

Jack showed his friend his prototype: it was a normal Frisbee, but attached to the

middle of the disc was a pair of model
helicopter blades.

"It's remote-
controlled," he
explained.

Oscar jumped to his feet. "Brilliant. Let's go
to the park. You can fix up my skateboard
and then we can test drive your remote-
control Frisbee. OK?"

Jack nodded and then looked concerned
as Oscar started to climb out of the window.

"Where are you going?" he asked.

Oscar turned and grinned. "You're not the
only one who can come up with brilliant
ideas you know. I thought we should have an
emergency exit, so I fixed up this zip line."
Now Oscar could see there was a cable
running from the tree house to Oscar's house.
Jack watched in fascination as Oscar clipped
a karabiner to the line, grabbed the rope

running through it and slid off down the zip wire.

Jack looked at where the zip wire was connected and made a rapid mental calculation. He started to call out a warning but it was too late.

SPLAT! Oscar slammed into the side of his house and dropped into the muddy flowerbed below.

"Just a few technical hitches to iron out," Oscar croaked weakly, before falling back into the squelchy mud.

CHAPTER TWO

Jack made some final adjustments to the makeshift ramp and stood up, brushing his hands together with satisfaction. He'd found a couple of bits of wood and some bricks in a skip on the way and had put them together to form a jump at the bottom of the largest slope in the park.

Jack looked up at the top of the hill where Oscar was waiting. Oscar waved his hand, enthusiastically.

This isn't going to go well, thought Jack.

He had insisted that Oscar put on some protective gear. Oscar, of course, didn't have any. So Jack had produced some of his own design that he had been working on. Adapted from swimming floats, the knee and elbow protectors were inflatable and as Oscar stood at the top of the hill, wearing the gear and the foam-lined strap-on yellow hard-hat that Jack had also made, he looked like a badly-dressed superhero from an old TV programme.

At Oscar's feet was the now-rocket-powered skateboard. Before they had left home Jack had found two old lemonade bottles in one of his 'Useful Materials' boxes and these were now firmly taped to the sides of the skateboard. Fixed to the centre of the board was an old foot pump with twin rubber pipes connecting it to both fuel tanks.

"Pump!" shouted Jack, after checking that the path at the bottom of the hill was clear of dog-walkers and other park users.

Oscar frantically pumped with his right foot, rapidly filling the bottles with air. The bottles began to swell, the plastic straining. Oscar kept pumping. Something would have to give. If Jack had made a mistake in his calculations the plastic would rupture and Oscar would end up – not for the first time – on his bottom. If Jack was *right*, the corks he had wedged into the bottle tops would be expelled like bullets from a gun, propelling the skateboard – and Oscar – forward at great speed.

POP! The two corks blew at exactly the same moment and Oscar's jet-powered skateboard launched on its maiden voyage.

Oscar came hurtling down the hill with his

arms outstretched to balance. The launch velocity had given him a much faster than usual start and now, as the board careered down the path, it picked up even more speed.

Oscar let out a cry that could have been excitement or fear (or possibly both). Moving at maximum speed, he hit the ramp.

Thrown violently into the air, he threw his arms back behind him, like the ski-jumpers he had seen on the Winter Olympics. Jack watched with a mixture of awe and pride as, for a long glorious moment, Oscar flew through the air. *It worked!* he thought.

But then he had another thought. *What about landing?*

At that moment, gravity woke up and remembered about Oscar. Jack had to cover his eyes as his friend returned rapidly to earth. Luckily, he landed in a bush, which absorbed the impact like one of the gym mats at school.

Unluckily, it was a rose bush.

"Ow!" said Oscar, picking thorns out of his bum. And then, more enthusiastically, "Wow! How cool was that?"

"Why don't you ever learn?" asked Jack, helping Oscar disentangle himself from the hedge. "You always crash when you do stuff like this."

Oscar grinned. "Yeah but the bit just before the crashes – that's awesome!" He dusted himself down and noticed that one of the inflatable arm bands had burst on impact. "And your safety gear was brilliant."

Stripping off Jack's now deflated limb protectors – and the helmet – Oscar stowed them all in his bag and turned to Jack.

"How about that Frisbee thing now?"

At the very moment that Oscar was climbing out of the bush, a grey squirrel appeared on the path nearby. Neither of the boys saw it. If they *had* seen it they may have noted that it was acting rather oddly. Rather than

scurrying across the path between trees like normal squirrels it was sitting perfectly still and looking around like an automated security camera scanning a car park. There was a very good reason for this – as anyone who looked closely at the squirrel's eyes would know. Because they *were* cameras.

There was a mechanical hum as the mysterious robot squirrel moved forwards to get a better view. Then it scanned the park and zoomed in on the boys as they began to play with the remote-control toy.

Nearby, a man watched carefully as the images from the Squirrel-Cam were fed back to his monitor. Could these boys be the ones he was looking for? They had courage, certainly, and ingenuity too. Both qualities the Watcher needed in any recruit. He sent a signal to the squirrel. Focus on the two boys. Follow them…

The heli-frisbee proved to be a great success. It was flying like a dream. The boys each took turns with the remote control and practised swooping it around, taking it low to the ground and then back up into the sky again. At one point when Oscar was at the controls it almost took the head off a rather dense squirrel that seemed mesmerised by the boys' activity. The heli-frisbee flew right at the poor creature, but all it did was stand there as still as a statue, looking at the device.

At the very last moment Jack managed to push the creature out of the way, saving it from decapitation.

Interesting, thought the Watcher from his secret hiding place. *Very interesting.*

"No, no, no," shouted Jack suddenly.

Oscar looked over at him, alarmed. "What's up?" he asked.

"The heli-frisbee," answered Jack.

"Well, duh, of course it is!"

"No, I mean it's *too far* up!" explained Jack. "If it gets too high in the sky it'll go out of range and…"

Oscar frowned, then frantically jigged the controls. "It's not responding!"

Jack sighed. "And we won't be able to control it."

He took the controls and had a go but it was no use. The boys watched helplessly as the heli-frisbee flew off over the bush – which still bore an Oscar-shaped imprint from his recent impact.

"Wait here with the other stuff," Jack shouted and bolted off.

Following the heli-frisbee, Jack ran along the fence until he found a gap leading into the ornamental gardens. Jack continued his pursuit, taking care to stick to the paths and not to damage any of the flowers. He didn't

notice a squirrel taking a more direct route through the flowerbeds behind him.

The heli-frisbee was beginning to lose height – it only just managed to clear the fence on the other side of the garden. Jack burst through another gap in the fence and stopped dead. A group of older kids, three or four of them, were bunched together in front of him. They had their backs to him. Something about the way they were standing troubled Jack. *What are they looking at?* he wondered. Then one of them moved and Jack could see the object of their attention.

It was a girl of about Jack's age. Jack didn't know much about girls; as a rule he tried not to have much to do with them. They confused him with their talk about things he had little interest in – boy bands, fashion, toy ponies – and this one looked like any other that he had come across. She had long black hair, pulled back in a pony tail, brown skin and bright intelligent blue eyes. She was also wearing a bright pink ballet dress thing... What was it called? A tutu? It was this distinctive and unusual fashion choice that had attracted the older kids' attention.

"Nice dress," said one of the older kids. Now Jack recognised her. It was Jess, a heavily-built girl from the nearby estate. When Jack and Oscar had started at primary school she had been in Year Six and everyone knew that she was a horrible bully. Jack realised that he was looking at the back of Jess's latest gang.

"Give us a twirl then," said Jess and the other kids laughed, and not in a nice way. "How about showing us some ballet?" Jess pronounced the word in the wrong way, sounding the final "t" to rhyme with jet.

The dark-haired girl just looked at them – her face set.

"I didn't *choose* this dress," she replied bravely. "Ballet's rubbish."

Jessica laughed. "In that case maybe we'd better put you in the bin."

Jack saw that there was a large rubbish bin further along the path. He didn't remember ever seeing it before. It was bigger than the usual park bins. The gang started milling around the tutu girl, pushing her towards the new bin.

"Hey, leave her alone!" said a boy's voice. In fact, Jack was surprised and a little worried to realise that it was *his* voice!

Jessica turned to look at him and Jack swallowed hard. Jess was even bigger – and scarier – than she'd been back in Year Six.

"Or what?" she demanded. Jess took a few steps towards Jack. Suddenly he heard a familiar buzzing sound. The heli-frisbee was spiralling downwards. WHACK!

It barrelled into the back of Jess's head and she fell forwards, squealing in shock. The older kids laughed at the very girlish sound that the usually tough Jess had just made.

Jack held up the remote control and pressed a button, hoping he was now in range. The heli-frisbee responded and flew up into the air again.

"You want some more?" he asked. The heli-frisbee had hit Jess by pure accident, but he figured it wouldn't be smart to let the bully know that.

Jess got to her feet. "I don't play with kids' toys," she sneered at him, then started to

walk off. "Come on," she ordered her gang, who seemed a little less in awe of her now. But slowly, they followed her. As the older kids wandered off, Jack was left alone with the tutu-wearing girl.

"Well, aren't you the hero?" she said sarcastically. "I could have taken them, you know."

Jack stared at her, not sure what to say. Then to his relief Oscar appeared, clutching his rocket-powered skateboard.

"Hey – where's the heli-frisbee?" he asked.

Moments later his question was answered as the remote-controlled flying machine flew into his back and knocked him to the ground.

The girl burst out laughing, and turned to Jack. "Sorry about that," she said. "I *am* grateful, really. It's just that I can handle myself. My name's Ruby, by the way."

Jack politely introduced himself and Oscar,

who was grumpily getting to his feet.

"Nice to meet you," said Ruby, "now, any chance I can have a go on that skateboard?"

CHAPTER THREE

The boys exchanged a look and then turned back to Ruby. She frowned and looked down at herself.

"Oh, it's the tutu, isn't it?" she sighed. "You think a girl in a tutu can't be interested in a super-charged skateboard."

"Well yeah," shrugged Jack. "Sort of."

Ruby laughed. "I'm only wearing this to make my mum think I've been to a ballet class," she explained.

"And… you *haven't* been to a ballet class?" asked Oscar, trying to keep up.

"No way – ballet sucks," retorted Ruby. "I've been to the pool for high-diving class. I go every night at five. My coach thinks I could dive at the 2012 Olympics."

"But your mum doesn't know about the lessons?" asked Jack.

"She'd freak. 'Too dangerous'. But according to her doing just about anything is really dangerous."

Oscar grinned. Ruby was speaking his kind of language.

"Come on then, let's get these rockets refilled," he suggested, "and we'll give you a go."

Jack watched Oscar and Ruby heading back towards the hill and the ramp. He walked over to the crashed Frisbee.

"Excuse me?" said a voice from somewhere behind him.

Jack whirled round. There was no one in sight.

"Who said that?" he asked.

"In here," said the voice again. It sounded slightly hollow and appeared to be coming from the new bin. Cautiously, Jack approached it.

"Am I talking to a rubbish bin?"

"My name is Bob," said the voice.

"A bin called Bob?"

"I'm Bob, I'm in the bin, but that's enough

about me, let's talk about you. You are a hero!"

Jack shook his head. "No, that's not quite right."

"The female said so. Listen."

There was a pause and then a recording of Ruby's voice emerged from the bin. "Aren't you the hero?" There was a click and then the mysterious voice was back. "The squirrel recorded everything."

"What squirrel?" asked Jack, his head beginning to spin now with the weirdness of the situation.

"Never mind that now. The point is we need heroes in GUNGE."

Suddenly the penny dropped for Jack. This must be some kind of set-up for a TV programme! Any minute now hidden cameras would reveal themselves and some grinning buffoon of a children's TV presenter would bound up and call him a good sport. And then... gunge him?!

"Oh, no – you're not sliming me. Not even if I do get to be on TV!" he exclaimed.

"No, you don't understand. I'm talking about GUNGE – the General Under-Committee for the Neutralisation of Gruesome Extraterrestrials," explained Bob.

"Extraterrestrials?"

"Yes. Aliens."

"You're an alien?" asked Jack.

"No. I work for GUNGE. We're a government agency dedicated to protecting Earth from the alien threat."

"What's the alien threat?"

"Invasion," said Bob.

"Ah." Jack's jaw dropped open. Alien invasion! This was bigger than any TV stunt, this was totally crazy.

"I want you to join GUNGE," said Bob. "Come

back when it gets dark, I'll explain everything to you then."

"Sure. Whatever," muttered Jack, convinced that this was either some kind of elaborate joke or the mutterings of a seriously deranged lunatic who'd got himself stuck in a bin. He gathered up the heli-frisbee and headed off back towards the hill.

When he got there he found a small crowd of kids, who had gathered to watch Ruby make her first attempt. As he joined them Ruby set off from the top of the hill, an odd sight in her pink tutu and Oscar's blow-up limb protectors. Unlike Oscar, Ruby shifted her balance on the board as she reached the ramp and her flight was more controlled. She hung in the air for a long moment and then landed perfectly, screeched to a halt and flicked the skateboard up with her heel and caught it one-handed.

The crowd clapped. "Awesome!" said Oscar. He paused. "Now tell me how you did it."

Seeing the other kids all applauding his new friend, Jack felt a little jealous. How was it that other people got to be good at stuff? If only Bob the Bin was right – it would be great to be a hero for a change. There and then Jack made a decision – he would go back later and see what the mysterious Bob was on about. Maybe this could be his thing? Maybe this time *he* could be the adventurous one?

Ruby made her way through the crowd to speak to Jack.

"Hey, Oscar said you made this thing, right?" Jack nodded.

"So how about adding a thrust engine to give more lift?"

"Like a booster at launch?"

"Yeah?" Ruby looked at him hopefully.

Jack smiled. "Yeah – why not."

Later, after Jack had eaten his tea, he told his mum a little white lie. "I have to go and work on a project with Oscar," he said. Mum just asked him not to be too late. Jack didn't like lying to his Mum but he had this feeling that telling her he was going to meet a talking rubbish bin named Bob, to discuss a secret organisation for getting rid of aliens, might land him in a lot of trouble.

When he reached the park it was already getting dark. The main gates were closed and chained up but Oscar had shown Jack a secret entrance. A little way along from the main gates a couple of the metal uprights in the fence were bent and a smallish child could squeeze through. Jack hurried through the now empty park to the place he had met Bob. In the moonlight the park was quite spooky.

"Excellent," said the now familiar tones of Bob as he approached. "I am glad you came back. Now listen carefully, I have much to tell you."

Jack sat down on the nearby park bench and tried to get comfortable.

Bob began by explaining that he was a member of a top secret agency dedicated to monitoring aliens and preventing alien invasion.

"Codenamed GUNGE," Jack speculated.

"Yes," replied Bob. "Now, there is another organisation known as GUNK—"

"GUNK?"

"The Galactic Union of Nasty Killer Aliens," explained Bob patiently.

Jack leant forward, frowning. "But there's no "A" in GUNK. So shouldn't it be just 'Galactic Union of Nasty Killer'?"

"The A is silent," Bob told him sharply. "And invisible. Like the K at the beginning of 'banana'"

"There *is* no K at the beginning of 'banana'," retorted Jack.

"Exactly," said Bob with satisfaction. "Now listen carefully and try not to interrupt. The thing is, the alien alliance known as GUNK use an... *unusual* energy source to power their technology. They use snot."

"*Snot?*"

"Yes. Snot. It is renewable, it is completely carbon neutral, and it is clean. Well, clean-*ish.*"

"But—"

"Please – no more interruptions."

"Sorry."

Suddenly a bright light shot out of the bin and Jack was forced to close his eyes. When he opened them again he wasn't in the park any more – he was in deep space!

"What the—"

"I *said*, no more interruptions!"

Jack saw that the bin was floating next to him in space.

"But I'm in space!" complained Jack. "How can I breathe?"

"This is an illusion – a 4D hologram," explained Bob. "I need to show you what we're up against."

Jack swallowed and tried to calm down. He wasn't floating in space really, it was just an illusion – but it felt so real. He could see stars and distant planets. And a spaceship, gleaming silver in the starlight.

As he watched, the ship drew nearer. It was pointy and menacing, with bulging weapon-bays.

"That is a GUNK scout ship," Bob told him. "Powered, of course, by snot. Ships like this one have been dispatched to every corner of the known universe on a mission to find human beings. You see, GUNK are starting to run out of their power source."

"They're running out of snot?" asked Jack, as he floated next to the sleek-hulled spaceship.

"Exactly. Now turn around."

Jack twisted, turning slowly in space as if he was underwater. He gasped. The ship was approaching a very familiar-looking planet.

Earth!

"Oh, no!" said Jack. "They're coming here!"

"Actually, this happened three weeks ago," said Bob. "They're already here. And if we don't do anything, they'll be taking our snot before you can say 'alien adventure'."

Jack nodded. "So… you want to stop them stealing our snot?"

"Yes."

"Why? I mean, I'm not that bothered about my snot. Oscar

51

would be upset – he likes to eat his. But we don't really need it, do we?"

Bob sighed. "Unfortunately, it is a little worse than you imagine."

Suddenly, the ship and the earth disappeared, and Jack found himself floating over a dark, smoking planet. Then he was sucked down as the image zoomed in. Now he and the bin floated over a long line of unhappy-looking humans, queuing up in the grime and darkness to enter a massive building. Aliens with nasty-looking guns made sure that no one escaped.

Passing through the walls like a ghost, Jack went inside and saw hundreds and hundreds of humans – men, women and children – all hooked up to massive snot-milking machines that were sucking the snot out of their noses as soon as it formed. From the expressions on their faces, it didn't look at all pleasant.

"They're like cows being milked!" he exclaimed.

"Well, yes, except instead of cows it's people, and instead of milk it's snot, and instead of udders it's noses, but apart from that it's a very similar process."

"It looks horrible."

"It is. But there is just one hope," continued Bob.

The illusion changed again and now Jack was looking at the scout ship again as it approached Earth. He passed through the walls and found himself inside the cabin, looking at the crew. There were four aliens, and it looked like they all came from different races – they were different sizes, and one had tentacles while another had a shell like a snail's. One of them oozed noxious slime

and one of them was even covered in tiny hands.

"There are four alien races in GUNK," confirmed Bob, "and although they have formed this union for the purposes of securing new sources of snot they don't exactly get along."

Even without being able to hear a thing, Jack could see that the aliens were arguing with each other. Tentacles and arms were being waved around furiously and none of

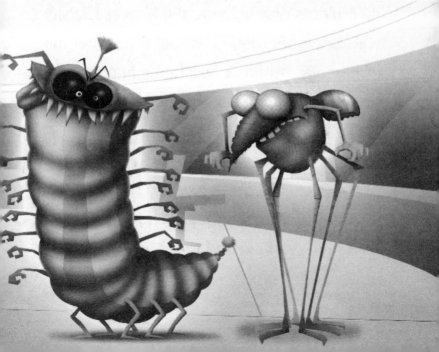

them seemed to be paying any attention to the control console where a red warning light was flashing.

"Basically they don't trust each other further than they can throw each other," Bob explained. "There's one representative from each race on each scout ship. Each one has one piece of the Blower – the trans-dimensional communicator they need to use to contact their home planets. It's like a beacon. As soon as these aliens combine their pieces and activate the blower, GUNK will know that they have found a planet full of humans. And they will home in on the signal and commence their invasion."

"So have they sent that signal?" asked Jack, alarmed.

"Not yet. The aliens were so busy with their petty argument that they missed a meteorite warning and their ship was damaged," said Bob.

Jack felt himself moving out of the scout-ship cabin and watched with a mixture of emotions as the ship was hit by a meteorite and span out of control towards the planet below.

"When it hit Earth's atmosphere the ship broke up," Bob told him. "The four aliens have been separated, along with their pieces of the Blower. They need to find each other and piece together the Blower before they can call in the invasion forces. We know that they have landed close to this town, and we have already safely disposed of their ship. But the aliens went into hiding, and we need help finding them. That's where you come in."

As quickly as the illusion had been created it ended and Jack was standing in the park again – talking to a bin.

"With your local knowledge, your bravery and your gadgets you are the perfect agent to take on this vital task," said Bob.

"No way!" exclaimed Jack.

"Yes way!" replied Bob. "Your mission is to find each alien, trap it and retrieve the portion of the Blower that they carry. Once we have all four pieces, we can be sure that they will be unable to call for assistance. And so GUNK will never know that we are here…"

"Piece of cake," said Jack, sarcastically.

"Go home now, get some sleep and be prepared."

"But I can't do this alone," Jack complained, "I'll need my friends, I'll need help."

"Go now," said Bob firmly, "I promise you – help will be with you soon."

cHAPTER FoUR

When Jack woke the next morning the
mysterious events in the park seemed
strangely distant – like they'd happened to
another person. *Was it all some kind of
weird dream?* he thought. He looked over at
his alarm clock. It said it was half past seven.
On a Sunday! Why was he
awake at that sort of hour on
a Sunday?

There was something scratching at the window. That's what had woken him – the scratching sound. *What was it?* Remembering Bob's dire warning, Jack had a sudden horrid thought – *was the sound at the window an alien coming to milk his snot?*

Carefully Jack slipped out of his bed and approached the window. Should he just pull back the curtain or should he peek? Maybe it wasn't an alien – maybe it was just Oscar. That was more likely.

"Oscar? Is that you?" Jack called out, hopefully.

There was no answer. Just the scratching, ever more frantic. Jack made a decision. If he was going to be a hero, if he was going to be an agent of GUNGE, he had to be brave. He reached out towards the curtain. As if sensing him coming closer whatever it was making the scratching noise suddenly stopped.

No going back now, Jack decided, and with a flurry he pulled open the curtains. At first he thought there was no one there – certainly no Oscar – but then he looked down at the window sill and saw the strangest-looking dog he had ever seen. The windows in Jack's room were the old-fashioned type which opened by sliding up and down so he quickly opened the window to let the dog – if it was a dog – in before it could fall. The creature bounded down into the room and leapt up onto his bed.

"What are you?" wondered Jack out aloud.

To his surprise the small furry creature answered him.

"I am Snivel – your Snot-Bot."

"A what-bot?"

"Snot-Bot. I am programmed to assist agents of GUNGE in dealing with alien invaders," explained the creature.

"Programmed?" repeated Jack. "You mean you're a robot?"

"Technically a canine-droid – a robot in the form of a dog," explained the creature. "I am a perfect copy of an average canine from Planet Earth. Correct to the last detail."

"Except for the eyes," Jack pointed out.

The dog bounded across the room to examine his reflection in the wardrobe mirror.

"Blue eyes are quite common among earth canines," he insisted.

"Yeah, that's probably true, but most dogs only have two."

Snivel looked at his reflection. As well as the two eyes either side of his nose there was a third on his face, sitting above the nose.

"My orders are to blend in and pretend to be your pet," he told Jack. "Will the third eye be a problem?"

Jack shook his head. "Mum's hardly ever around – she works really long shifts at the hospital – and when she is here she's too tired to notice much. But other people might. Can you keep that third eye shut without affecting the other two?"

Snivel tried to do just that but only succeeded in going cross-eyed and falling over.

"I may need to practise," he confessed.

Jack sat down on the bed and looked at his new pet. It was basically dog-like but somehow it was just a bit wrong. It looked a bit like a small terrier but one that had been made from spare parts. Its paws looked just a bit too big for its legs, its tail was just a bit too short, its ears just a bit too far apart. Nevertheless there was something rather appealing about it. As Jack watched, Snivel kept trying to close his third eye.

Every time he did it he fell over.

"Don't worry about it now," Jack told him kindly. "It won't be a problem when you're with me and my friends."

Snivel came over and sat on Jack's lap.

"Bob said something about trapping these aliens. How do I do that then?" Jack asked his new assistant.

"I can transform my shape to make a trap," explained Snivel. "All you have to do is say,

'Activate Snivel Trap'. Your voice wave patterns have already been programmed into my circuits."

Jack cleared his throat. This he had to see. "Activate Snivel Trap," he said. Before his astonished eyes, Snivel stood bolt upright and changed shape, turning into a flat-sided box with an open lid. As soon as he had stopped transforming the two lid flaps flipped shut with a resounding clunk. After a moment Snivel snapped back to his usual shape.

"Multi-functionality," he said proudly. "I help you sniff out the aliens and then I turn into the trap to hold them. Only snag is the alien has to be right on top of me when you give the command."

Jack was amazed. Oscar *had* to see this. He looked down at the Snot-Bot.

"I need my friend Oscar in

on this," he told the robot-dog. "Is that allowed?"

"Secrecy is important," said Snivel, "but you may involve trusted associates at your discretion."

"Don't worry – Oscar's very discreet," said Jack, crossing his fingers behind his back. "Let's go find him."

Half an hour later, after a quick breakfast, Jack was introducing Oscar to Snivel. Having had some time to get used to the idea of a three-eyed robotic pet/alien-trap Jack was able to enjoy the look of complete disbelief on Oscar's face.

For a moment it looked as if Oscar might never close his mouth. He just stood there looking at the robotic dog with his jaw hanging open.

"What's the matter, Oscar? Have you never seen a canine-droid before?"

"Awesome," muttered Oscar finally.

Jack decided to call the meeting to order. He had already explained everything that Bob had told him last night and everything that Snivel had told him this morning. Now was the time for action. They needed to track down these aliens before they had a chance to find each other and put together the Blower.

Snivel touched his nose and a beam of light shot out from his third eye, forming a 3-D hologram that hung in the air. The hologram showed an image of an alien. It looked like a mutant offspring of an octopus and a jellyfish – with a bloated head like a balloon filled with snot, and countless tentacles all covered with sucker plates. Five eyes stuck into the air on stalks. They wobbled in the breeze.

"This is a Squillibloat," announced Snivel.

"One of the four aliens that were on board the rocket which crash landed here. We believe he has the main chip for the Blower,

and so he is the priority-one target. We must catch him soon, before he can find his friends, or *they* find him."

"And how are we supposed to find him first?" asked Jack.

Oscar snorted. "Something that ugly won't be hard to find."

them. "It has a disguise unit that will help it blend in. It will look like a human. Roughly, anyway. But the disguise unit is very energy inefficient – it will need constant fuelling with human snot."

"So… the alien will be somewhere where there are

69

lots of people around?" said Jack.

"Yes. And we can narrow it down further. He will seek out a habitat similar to his home planet," said Snivel. "He comes from an ocean-covered planet and loves warm water. He feeds on algae and fungus."

Jack and Oscar considered for a moment. Then they both looked at each other. *Lots of people, water, algae...*

"The pond at the park!" they said in unison.

Twenty minutes later the two boys were in the park. The pond was at the bottom of the hill on the opposite side from the ornamental gardens. As they approached they saw a figure close to the pond, using an old-fashioned rake to scrape the fallen leaves into a pile.

Jack turned to Snivel. "Could that be him?"

Snivel shrugged, which is hard to do in a dog's body. "Impossible to say at this distance."

"He's hanging around the pond," reasoned Oscar, "and he's got a constant supply of people visiting the park…"

Yes, the more they looked, the more this man with his rake seemed suspicious.

"I mean, why does he need to put the leaves in a pile anyway?" said Oscar. "He's obviously faking."

Jack looked around for something they could use. He spotted a net rolled up at the side of the tennis courts. Perfect. Quickly, he outlined a plan to Oscar and Snivel.

Snivel went bounding off, running directly into the pile of leaves that the mysterious stranger was raking. The man – or alien – gave out an angry roar and began chasing after the dog. His mouth hung open and he drooled a little with the effort of running.

Definitely looks like an alien, thought Jack. *This GUNGE agent stuff is easy!*

Snivel was too fast for the alien-man-thing, though, and hurried back the way he came. The man followed and ran straight into the net which Oscar and Jack had stretched across the path. Quickly they ran rings around the man, wrapping him tightly until they ran out of net. The creature – now tightly bound by netting – fell over.

Carefully Oscar, Jack and Snivel approached the prone figure.

"What do you hooligans think you're doing?" it spluttered furiously. "I'm the council park-keeper assigned to this recreation facility and you are both in serious trouble."

Jack ignored the man and looked to Snivel. "Can you scan him?"

The dog nodded and a moment later shook his head. "Not alien," he announced.

"Not alien?" repeated the man, who was unable to see Snivel from his position lying on the ground and had assumed that it was one of the boys speaking. "Of course I'm not alien. I come from Lincoln."

Oscar and Jack exchanged quick looks. "Leg it," suggested Oscar. Jack nodded. They ran.

cHAPTER FIVE

After the excitement at the park the rest of
Sunday went rapidly downhill for Jack. He
and Oscar had run for their lives, with Snivel
at their heels, and then they had gone to
Oscar's house to get a sandwich.

Back at the tree house, they spent a long
time studying a local map, looking for other
watery locations that might be appealing to
the Squillibloat. The best they could come up

with was the canal that ran through the town but, as Snivel pointed out, that was likely to be cold water rather than warm.

"Why didn't you mention that before we rushed off to the pond in the park?" complained Jack. "That water's not exactly toasty either!"

"Hey, I'm not perfect you know," replied Snivel in a hurt voice. Jack looked at him. His third eye blinked, and one of his ears was sticking up at an unusual angle.

"Well," said Jack. "You're right about *that*."

Snivel went back to trying – and failing – to close his third eye.

The boys decided to sleep on the problem and both went home. When Jack opened the door his mother called out from the kitchen. "Jack – come here please." Jack knew that tone of voice.

When Mum used that tone

of voice, you were in *real* trouble.

"Quick – go up to my room," he whispered to Snivel and then headed for the kitchen. Mum looked at him and shook her head sadly. This was bad. She was still dressed in her nurse's uniform and Jack realised with horror that she was back from work early.

"I got a visit at work," she began, "from the police. They'd had a complaint from a park-keeper about two boys attacking him."

Jack swallowed hard. This was not going anywhere good.

Mum produced something from her bag – it was the hard-hat. Inside he could see the legend 'Property of Jack Brady' written with permanent marker. For a split second Jack considered telling his mum the truth but then he came to his senses. Instead he muttered something about it being a game that had got out of hand.

"You're lucky," his mum told him. "The park-keeper is not going to press charges but you're not getting off scot-free. You, young man, are Grounded!"

Oh, no. When Mum pronounced words with capital letters at the start, you were in *real, real* trouble.

Jack glanced up at her face and tried to look sheepish. Mum was adamant though. And there was more. "Where's the dog?" she asked. "The park-keeper said you had a dog with you, and I know it's not Oscar's. His mum told me he can't have pets, because his dad's allergic."

"I don't have a dog, Mum," Jack lied.

Just then, there was a snuffling sound from somewhere at their feet. Jack and his mum both looked towards the source of the sound. It was Snivel, half in and half out of the kitchen bin. In his mouth – a snotty tissue. Snivel realised that he had been spotted and stopped moving. Slowly the bin toppled over, depositing the Snot-Bot, some vegetable peelings and the left-overs from last night's Chinese take-away all over the kitchen floor.

Jack sent Snivel to his room and helped his mum clear up the mess.

"I found him on the streets. I think he's been abandoned," Jack told her. "Can't we keep him?"

Mum sighed. "We'll put an ad in the paper. It must have some owners somewhere... Oh Jack, your father would be so disappointed in you."

Jack said nothing. Mum didn't mention his father very often. His dad had left home when he was very little. The exact reason for him going was never very clear but it had something to do with getting a job in a toilet paper factory in Sweden. Jack hadn't seen his dad for over five years. As far as Jack was concerned if there was any disappointing being done it was by his dad not him!

With the mess cleared up Jack made it back to his room. "What were you doing?" he asked Snivel. "I told you to come here, not go to the kitchen."

"I needed that tissue," explained Snivel. "I run on snot."

Jack took a step back,

nervously. "I thought it was *alien* technology that ran on snot."

"Ah. Well, yes, that's true. The thing is, the aliens are a bit more advanced than we are when it comes to robotics. GUNGE salvaged some parts from a GUNK rocket that crash-landed on Mars. And I'm the result! But don't worry – I've been completely re-programmed. I don't have *any* urges to enslave humankind any more."

"Um… OK," said Jack. "So… you eat snot?"

Snivel wagged his tail (he got it slightly wrong: dogs are supposed to wag their tails from side to side, not up and down). "Yes. It's delicious."

Jack wrinkled his face in disgust. Snivel's ears pricked up.

"Are you about to sneeze? If you could just lean over and direct it at me…"

Monday morning was grey and bleak. Well, it was for Jack. In reality it was a lovely sunny autumnal day, with a crisp cool wind scattering the red and brown fallen leaves from the trees that lined the road to school. For Jack though, after the excitement of the weekend, it was back to normal with a bump.

The school day dragged on in what felt like slow motion. Finally it was time to go home. Still feeling miserable, Jack headed for his house. Grounded! With a capital G! It was so unfair. Knowing that he wouldn't be allowed out again once he got home Jack deliberately dawdled and took the long route home.

"Hey, Jack," someone shouted, cutting into his bleak mood. He looked up and saw someone wearing a ball-gown walking towards him.

It was Ruby. "Ballroom dancing lessons," she explained with a wink, "at least that's what Mum thinks. Of course I'm really going to the pool. But not to dive… that's boring."

Jack wondered how anyone could speak so fast without stopping to breathe.

"You know the pool's got this awesome new wave machine, so now they're doing surfing. They have boards there, and everything, so you don't even need your own. I mean, obviously, because, you know, if I had a surfboard on me you'd see it, wouldn't you?"

She stopped and it seemed that Jack was required to contribute something to the conversation.

"Right," he said, keeping it simple.

"Have you ever tried surfing?" she asked excitedly.

"No," he replied with a heavy sigh.

Ruby bristled. "Well, pardon me for existing. I can see you've better things to do than talk to me..." She pushed past Jack and hurried off down the street. Jack turned and watched her. *What did I do wrong there?* He shook his head and made his way home.

A little bit later the encounter with Ruby was still running through Jack's head. He was meant to be doing his homework but with Snivel's computer brain at his disposal he had finished that in record time. Now he was thinking about the Squillibloat again. He looked at the map and absent-mindedly traced his route home from school to the point where he'd run into Ruby. Who'd talked to him about...

A wave machine.

Surfing.

THE SWIMMING POOL!

Of course, lots of people, warm water, it was the obvious place for the alien to be. Quickly he told Snivel his theory. After he had explained exactly what a swimming pool was, the Snot-Bot agreed that it was a likely location. They had to get there as soon as possible.

There was just one problem.

He was Grounded.

With a capital G.

cHApTER sIx

Jack looked at the drainpipe outside his window and then down at the ground. It seemed an awfully long way away. Oscar was always telling him to use it to get out but then Oscar seemed to *enjoy* falling off things. Jack didn't mind the idea of falling off things – he just didn't like the notion of hitting the ground afterwards.

"Jump!" Snivel encouraged him.

"I was thinking about climbing down the drainpipe, not jumping!" replied Jack. "I don't want to break my legs." His mum was watching TV downstairs, so there was no way he could go out the front door.

"Sorry – I forget how fragile you humans are," said Snivel before leaping right out of the window past Jack, somersaulting in the air and then landing with bent knees on the lawn.

"Come on then," he called up at his human 'owner'.

Not quite believing what he was doing Jack climbed out of his bedroom window and grabbed hold of the drainpipe. It was an old metallic pipe, quite wide and solid. Slowly, with his eyes shut, Jack edged down while Snivel called out what were probably meant to be words of encouragement.

"Come on! The Ning-Nongs of Bute 3 would have been down that drainpipe in a matter of seconds," Snivel told him. "Of course the Ning-Nongs have sixteen arms and a sticky belly but that's beside the point."

Finally Jack made it to solid ground. He felt really proud. He had conquered his fear. Sadly, his only witness was an alien canine-droid. Jack hurried to fetch Oscar and tell him his theory. Oscar listened carefully and agreed that the swimming pool was an obvious place to find the Squillibloat.

"You know I've had to get my head around a lot of weird stuff this last couple of days," Oscar told Jack as they set off, "but I can't believe you actually came down the drainpipe!"

Jack sighed.

Snivel told them what they should be looking for at the pool. "Keep your eyes peeled for someone a bit odd, someone who doesn't eat human food but loves fungus and doesn't get too far away from the water," he advised.

Jack and Oscar assured him that they understood. They turned a corner and almost ran directly into Ruby. She was still wearing the ballroom dress.

"Oh, it's you," she said, a bit snootily. "I didn't know you had a dog."

"His name's Snivel," said Oscar, trying to be friendly.

"It's got three eyes," she said, suspiciously.

"I thought you were going to the pool?" asked Jack, changing the subject.

"It was closed earlier for cleaning but it should be open again now. I'm on my way to surf practice."

"We're going there too," Oscar told her, unaware of Jack vigorously shaking his head behind Ruby's back.

"I'll come with you," she said, smiling.

"No, don't worry," Jack told her. "In fact I wouldn't bother to go. I heard on the radio that it was still closed."

Jack, Oscar and Snivel hurried off, taking the nearby alley which was sign-posted 'Swimming Pool'.

Ruby, hands on her hips, eyes narrowed, watched them

go. *If the pool's really closed then why are* they *going there?*

At the pool there was a public gallery where parents who didn't want to swim could sit and watch their children splashing about in safety. The parents knew their kids were safe because there was a lifeguard on duty, sitting on a tall chair overlooking the pool.

Hiding Snivel in a sports bag, Jack and Oscar paid for two gallery tickets and took up positions on the benches to check out the pool. It was quiet with not too many people in at the moment. Most of the swimmers looked to be kids. One girl strayed into the deep end and began to flounder, splashing around. The lifeguard got to his feet and went to help her.

Jack nudged Oscar. "Look – the lifeguard."

Oscar looked. He drew in a breath.

There was *definitely* something odd about the man. Usually, lifeguards were quite fit, young people but this one looked a bit... bulgy. He was wearing a one-piece wetsuit but it jutted out strangely in all sorts of places, making him look like a plastic bag jammed full of rubber balls.

Jack pulled a pair of binoculars from his bag and took a closer look. He focused in. As the lifeguard lifted the girl out of the water something strange happened. A snake like tentacle appeared out of his sleeve, just for a moment, and licked the girl's foot.

Jack told Oscar what he had just seen and passed him the binoculars. Over the next ten minutes they watched the same scenario play out again and again. The lifeguard was the alien they were looking for. And it was eating people's veruccas!

Snivel took a look too and confirmed their theory. "See that weird necklace he's wearing?" he asked. The boys hadn't really noticed it before but the lifeguard-alien-thing did have something glowing around his neck. "That's his bit of the Blower!"

Jack looked around. Too many people around to do anything now.

"There's no way he can stray too far from the water," Snivel told them. "He'll have to be here all night."

"Then we'll have to come back later," announced Jack. "Don't worry – I have a plan!"

They got up to go. As they shuffled towards the exit they could see Ruby – now in a bathing suit – starting her surfing lesson. Oscar gave her a friendly wave but she turned her head away and ignored him.

"Girls," commented Jack, shaking his head. "I reckon aliens are easier to understand than girls!

CHAPTER SEVEN

Jack explained his plan on the way back to the tree house. Oscar and Snivel listened carefully.

"The key is the verrucas," he explained. "The Squillibloat needs them. So that's his weakness."

"We need a verruca bazooka!" joked Oscar, pleased with his rhyme.

"That'll be us – the ultimate weapon against the Squillibloat," said Jack determinedly, "and this is how we'll do it..."

At the tree house they collected the materials and gadgets they needed for Jack's plan. Then they made their way back to the swimming pool. It was nearly closing time but they told the woman on reception that they'd left something in the changing room earlier and they were allowed to go back in. Inside, they left Snivel hidden in the changing room and then left the building along with all the other swimmers. No one paid them any special attention – except for one pair of eyes.

One solitary observer watched the boys enter the male changing rooms with the bag containing Snivel, and then watched them emerge later *without* the bag. The watching eyes narrowed suspiciously and the mind behind them made a decision…

Outside the swimming pool Jack and Oscar lay in the shadow of the trees that lined the car park and waited. When the last swimmers had left they got up and approached the rear emergency exit of the pool. The doors opened and there was Snivel, letting them in exactly on time. The boys hurried inside. In the changing room Oscar quickly got into his swimming trunks. At the same time Jack fitted the doggy scuba kit to Snivel. Finally Jack fixed some special fake verrucas he had made using modelling clay to the soles of Oscar's feet. Oscar looked down at the green blobs on his feet. "Ugh," he said. "They look rank."

"Thanks," said Jack. "I reckon the Squillibloat won't be able to resist them!"

Preparations complete they headed for the pool. Oscar got into the water and immediately began to splash around as if in trouble. Jack and Snivel found a place to hide behind a cupboard of floats. As they had hoped, the lifeguard heard the noise and came running. At the poolside he hesitated. He looked around. The building was empty. Maybe he didn't *have* to save this human. Who would know?

Jack whispered urgently to Snivel. "How do we know it'll bother to save him?"

"I don't know," replied Snivel. "It's your plan."

"Thanks for your help," snapped Jack. The alien was still just standing at the side of the pool watching the 'drowning' Oscar. "If he lets a kid drown he'll lose his job, and if he loses his job he'll lose access to the pool, and all the people and… all the veruccas!" Jack snapped his fingers. "Quick, into the pool," he ordered Snivel. "Make sure Oscar shows him his feet! And remember, you have to be right underneath the Squillibloat for the trap to work."

Snivel gave him a withering look. "I told you that in the first place," he said. "Silly human b—"

He was cut off by Jack slipping on his oxygen mask. "Who are you calling silly?" he said. "I'm not the dog in the scuba gear."

He pushed Snivel into the water. Breathing air from the silver tanks, the Snot-Bot swam submarine-style towards Oscar. Like a torpedo he rammed Oscar's back causing him to tumble backwards in the water, and shooting his feet clear of the surface.

Immediately the alien spotted the multitude of verrucas on the drowning boy's feet. And now it leapt into action. It wasn't going to let this opportunity go!

SPLASH!

In seconds the lifeguard-alien-thing was at Oscar's side, dragging him to the edge of the pool. As expected, a tentacle slithered out and sucked up one of Oscar's verrucas.

"Ugh!" said Oscar, shuddering. "What was that? Something touched my foot!"

"Probably a poo," announced the lifeguard

in a bizarre croaky voice. "Floating in the water. Human children can be *so* disgusting."

"Human! What do you mean human children?" asked Oscar, extending the conversation to create a diversion. Meanwhile Snivel swam into position underneath the alien.

Jack sensed his moment. Taking a deep breath, he broke cover and grabbed the necklace from around the lifeguard's neck. He needed to get hold of the Blower part before trapping the alien in the Snivel-trap.

He pulled with all his strength but the necklace refused to break free.

With a roar of anger the alien burst out of the lifeguard costume, revealing his true form. In the flesh the Squillibloat was even more disgusting than the hologram had suggested. Six of its larger tentacles wrapped around Oscar and pulled him under the water.

"Remove your hand from my property or I will drown your friend," roared the creature. Two of its upper tentacles wrapped themselves around Jack's legs. Jack began to panic – this wasn't going to plan at all. If only the alien had eaten more of the fake "veruccas"...

Suddenly there was a whoosh as the wave machine started up. *Who turned that on?* wondered Jack. But there was another development, too – the lower tentacles of the creature were now sucking up all the "veruccas" from Oscar's feet – Jack's special fake ones, made from modelling clay and laced with… chilli powder.

The waves were building up in strength now but the Squillibloat didn't seem to have noticed. It was turning bright red and gasping for breath.

"What… have… you done… to me…?" it gasped.

Jack felt the grip of the tentacles relax. Swivel was in position but if he activated the Trap now Oscar would get caught along with the alien. What to do?

Suddenly a solution appeared in the form of Ruby, surfing the waves like a professional.

"Surf's up!" she shouted, and as she flew past
them on her board she reached down and
pulled Oscar free.

Jack took his chance and yanked
backwards, pulling the necklace clear.
"Activate Snivel Trap!" he screamed. There
was a flash of blue light and a sound like a

thunderclap and suddenly the Squillibloat
was gone, sucked into the Snivel Trap which
now floated benignly on the surface of the
pool.

At the shallow end Oscar was getting to
his feet, helped by Ruby.

"You guys have got some serious
explaining to do," she said.

CHAPTER EIGHT

Ruby was amazed at their story but she couldn't ignore the evidence of her own eyes. She had spotted Snivel's third eye right away and the Squillibloat had been even harder to discount. She had to accept that the whole story, from talking bins to snot-stealing aliens, was true.

"But what about you?" asked Jack. "What were you doing here?"

Ruby explained about seeing them go into the changing rooms with the bag and then coming out without it. "I knew something was going on," she told them, "so I hid in the changing rooms to find out what. Good job I did, really."

Oscar thanked her again for saving him. Ruby looked around. "I wonder what happened to the real lifeguard?"

They made a quick search of the building and found him, covered in slime and locked in an equipment locker. They left the poor man looking for a shower and made their excuses. Somehow, without anyone saying anything, Ruby seemed to have become part of the team. Carrying the Snivel Trap between them, Jack and Oscar headed for the park and the bin containing Bob. Ruby walked with them, clutching the necklace.

Bob was delighted to see them. Ruby

thought it a bit odd that he stayed hidden in the bin, but when she questioned this he told her it was a security issue and it was important for their safety that he remain unseen. Ruby nodded and handed over the necklace.

"That's the first part of the Blower safely in our hands," Bob told them.

"And here's the Alien who had it," said Jack, placing the Snivel Trap in front of the bin.

A beam of bright blue light suddenly appeared from the bin, shining down onto the trap. The light seemed to… *wibble*. It was so bright Jack had to shield his eyes. Then suddenly the light vanished, as if someone had flicked an off-switch.

When Jack opened his eyes, Snivel was sitting there in his usual dog form, tail wagging happily.

He still had three eyes.

"Keep your eyes peeled for Snivel," Bob told them. "Next time you see him he'll have your next mission for you…"

And with that, the Snot-Bot jumped into the bin, and disappeared.

"Whoa," said Ruby. "Did you see that? It's like a rabbit and a hat, only it's a dog and a bin, and the dog vanished instead of appearing, because usually with a rabbit and a hat it's the rabbit that gets magicked out of the hat and—"

"Ruby?" said Jack.

"Yes?"

"Shut up."

Ruby looked shocked for a moment, then burst out laughing. Jack grinned. A couple of days ago he'd been a geeky inventor with only one friend. Now he was part of a gang – and best of all, he was a GUNGE agent!

There's just one more piece of unfinished business, thought Jack as he said goodbye to his friends and walked up the path towards his front door.

Mum.

He was meant to be Grounded. What on earth would she say when he came home now? He'd probably be Grounded until he collected his pension.

As he reached for the door knocker the door swung open and his mum was standing there in the doorway.

"Why did you lie to me, Jack?" she demanded.

Jack lowered his head in

shame. *Here it comes*, he thought, *the big shouty bit*.

But Mum didn't shout, instead she bent down and gave him a hug.

"You're a hero Jack! And you didn't even tell me!"

Jack looked at his mum, startled. *What on earth*? And then he realised. Of course –this didn't have anything to do with Earth. It had to be GUNGE. They'd told her about his work. He realised that his mum had the phone in her hand. She thrust it at him.

"The man from the RSPCA just told me all about it," she said, "and he said he wants to speak to you."

Jack took the phone and put it to his ear. RSPCA? Then he heard a familiar voice in his ear.

"Just go along with everything I say," said Bob. It was strange to hear his voice coming from a phone instead of a bin. Jack nodded and made the murmuring noise his mum always made when listening to someone on the other end of a phone.

Bob quickly filled Jack in on what he had told his Mum. The story was that Jack had rescued Snivel from a sack in the pond in the park. Some horrible man had tried to kill his dog but Jack's quick action had saved him. The business with the tennis net had been a well-intentioned attempt to catch the would-be dog killer, which had unfortunately trapped the park-keeper instead. And just this evening Jack had been at the vet's paying for vital injections that Snivel needed – from his own pocket money.

Jack thought the last detail might have been a bit too much; his pocket money would hardly stretch to much of a vet's bill, but his

mum was so pleased to be hearing such
positive things about her brave boy that she
never questioned a word.

"Just nod and say yes," instructed Bob.

Jack did as he was told and then hung up.
Immediately his mum gave him a huge hug.

Jack hoped none of his friends were passing and pushed the front door closed with his foot. As the door swung closed Snivel jumped through the gap.

Mum looked down at the canine-droid and sighed. "He's an odd-looking thing but if you promise to look after him, I guess we can keep him."

Jack grinned. "Thanks, Mum."

Mum started walking towards the kitchen.

"Now let's get you something to eat. My little hero..."

Snivel winked at him with his third eye. Boy and canine-droid shared the same thought: *she doesn't know the half of it...*

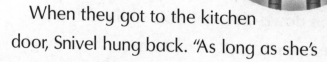

When they got to the kitchen door, Snivel hung back. "As long as she's getting *you* something to eat," he said, "do you reckon you could find a snotty tissue?"

Half a mile away, in the trans-dimensional weirdness that existed, impossibly, inside the bin, Bob the GUNGE agent walked along a dark corridor of glass-walled cells. One was lit up. Inside, the unconscious form of the Squillibloat lay on a bed. At the end of the corridor was a free-standing shelving unit with four individually lit platforms.

Bob placed the necklace that Jack had taken from the Squillibloat onto the first of the platforms. For a moment the necklace glowed with a spooky green light and then faded.

One down, thought Bob to himself with satisfaction. *And three to go.*

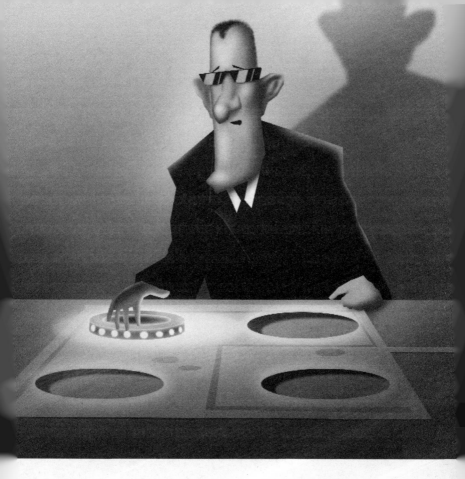

The Squillibloat had been fairly easy. They were not a race known for their intelligence. The boy and his friends had conducted themselves well, but the next mission would be far more of a test…

Bob walked back along the corridor. Soon, with Jack's help, all these cells would be occupied and the four bits of the Blower would be his. And then... well, then Earth would be safe and everything would be OK...

Wouldn't it?

Take a sneak peek at book 2 in the Gunk adventure!

The first part of the plan was the easiest. Getting into the actual elephant enclosure wasn't too difficult. Oscar's lock-picking soon had them through a gate which gave them access. As Jack had predicted, the crowds had hurried off to see feeding time with the penguins and, with no one around to watch them, most of the elephants had trudged inside.

The giant elephant that was of most interest to Jack and his friends was standing in one of the hay-filled bays, relaxing – exactly how they wanted him. Jack smiled at Ruby.

Oscar opened the bag of elephant treats and approached the giant pachyderm. "Here you are, Jumbo, just for you…" he said, holding the bag out. The elephant reached out with his trunk and took something from the bag. It was an apple. The elephant bent his trunk back and popped the apple into his mouth.

"Plenty more where that came from," offered Oscar, stroking the elephant's trunk with his other hand.

"Are you sure you're up for this?" Jack asked Ruby.

"Absolutely," she said with a grin. While Oscar kept the elephant occupied she quickly used her climbing skills to shimmy up the trunk and onto his head. From there she got herself into position on the elephant's shoulders. Now she could begin to reach down towards the ear where the mysterious earring was glowing.

Suddenly there was a horrified cry.

"Oy!" It was the elephant keeper, and he was standing in the doorway. With the terrifying sound of a plum splitting, but amplified about a thousand times, the alien abandoned its disguise, shedding and shredding his 'human' skin to reveal his true form. It was even worse in the flesh than it had been in Snivel's hologram projection. It was like looking at a giant insect, a bit like a cross between a house fly and a mosquito. Despite losing its human disguise it was still capable of speech.

"Get away from there, human half-grown!" it screeched in a high-pitched tone. "Or I will suck your friend dry."

Without warning it pounced on Oscar, pulling him to the ground.

Petrified, Oscar broke wind. The alien roared with delight. "Let the harvest begin!" it cried and thrust its head directly towards poor Oscar's bum.

While Jack looked on in horror, the alien took a deep breath and began to expand. Before his very eyes the Burrapong was getting bigger.

Oscar's cheeks were sucked in and his eyes bulged. A horrible squeal came from his mouth.

"It's vacuuming up his farts!" said Snivel. "All of them. We have to stop him before he pulls Oscar inside out!"

JONNY MOON

THEY CAME FROM SPACE   TO GET UP YOUR NOSE!

GUNK
ALIENS
THE DOG'S DINNER

THE THIRD GROSSLY FUNNY GUNK ALIENS ADVENTURE!

The gang face their toughest challenge yet, as they go after a terrifying flying alien. In an epic confrontation, Jack's inventing skills will be tested to the limit, one of his new friends will fall, and all of his courage will be needed when he takes on the worst ordeal of all. Eating a school dinner...

JOIN THE FIGHT IF YOU VALUE YOUR SNOT!

JONNY MOON

THEY CAME FROM SPACE   TO GET UP YOUR NOSE!

GUNK ALIENS
THE SEWERS CRISIS

THE FOURTH
GROSSLY FUNNY
GUNK ALIENS ADVENTURE!

Jack and his friends are nearing the end of their mission, with only one alien left to capture. The best is always saved for last, though, so none of them should be surprised that this particular alien loves only one thing… poo! But at least, once they've made a sickening descent into the sewers, the world should finally be safe. Shouldn't it?

JOIN THE FIGHT IF YOU VALUE YOUR SNOT!